MARC BROWN

ARTHUR'S TOOTH

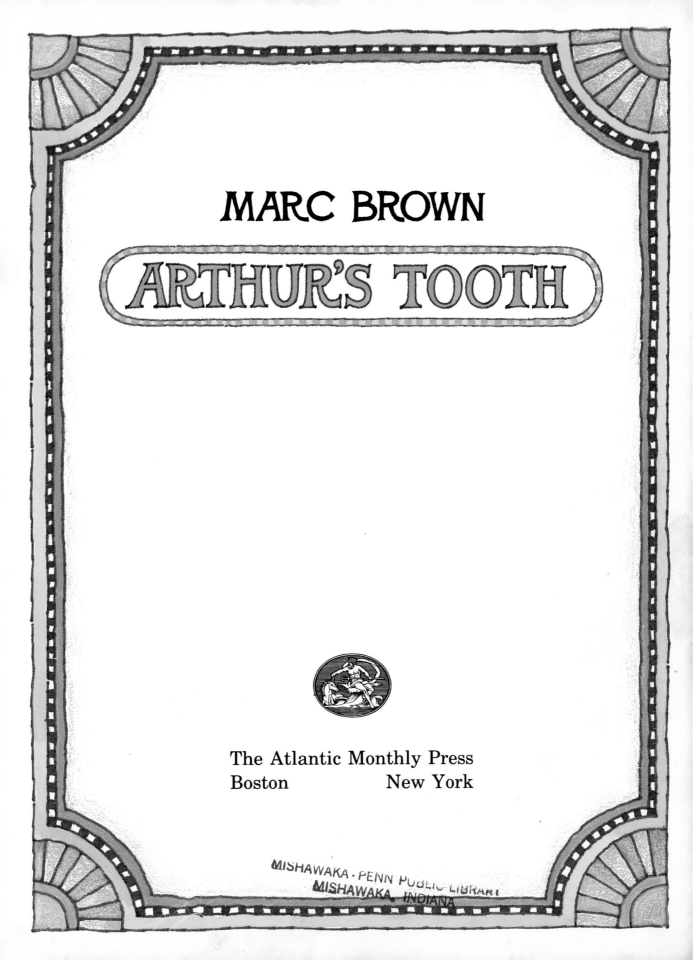

The Atlantic Monthly Press
Boston   New York

For Ralph Sozio, S.D. *(Super Dentist)*

FIRST EDITION

Library of Congress Cataloging in Publication Data

Brown, Marc Tolon.
  Arthur's tooth.

  Summary: Arthur, tired of being the only one in his class who still has all his baby teeth, waits impatiently for his loose tooth to fall out.
  1. Children's stories, American. [1. Teeth — Fiction]
I. Title.
PZ7.B81618Aru 1985   [E]   84-72092
ISBN 0-87113-006-8

WOR

Published simultaneously in Canada

PRINTED IN THE UNITED STATES OF AMERICA

Finally, Arthur had a loose tooth.
He wiggled it with his tongue.
He wiggled it with his finger.
He wiggled it all the time.

One afternoon while Arthur was wiggling his tooth during math, he heard a loud scream. Francine jumped up.

"My tooth just fell out on my desk!" she cried.
"Class, how many of you have lost a tooth?"
asked Mr. Marco.
Everyone but Arthur raised their hands.

When Arthur got home, he didn't want any milk and cookies.

"What's the matter, Arthur?" his mother asked.

"I'm the only one in my class who still has all his baby teeth," he complained.

"Don't worry," said his sister, D.W. "Before
you know it, all your teeth will fall out and
you can get false teeth like Grandma Thora."

Arthur persuaded Father to make a special
dinner for him: steak, corn on the cob, and
peanut brittle.
"I can't believe one little tooth can take
so long to fall out," said Father.

The next day, Muffy brought in a whole jar of her teeth for show-and-tell.

"I got two dollars for each one," she said.

"One from my dad and one from my mom. I put it all in the bank to earn interest. I'm waiting for my investment to double."

"Not me," said Francine. "I'm spending mine."

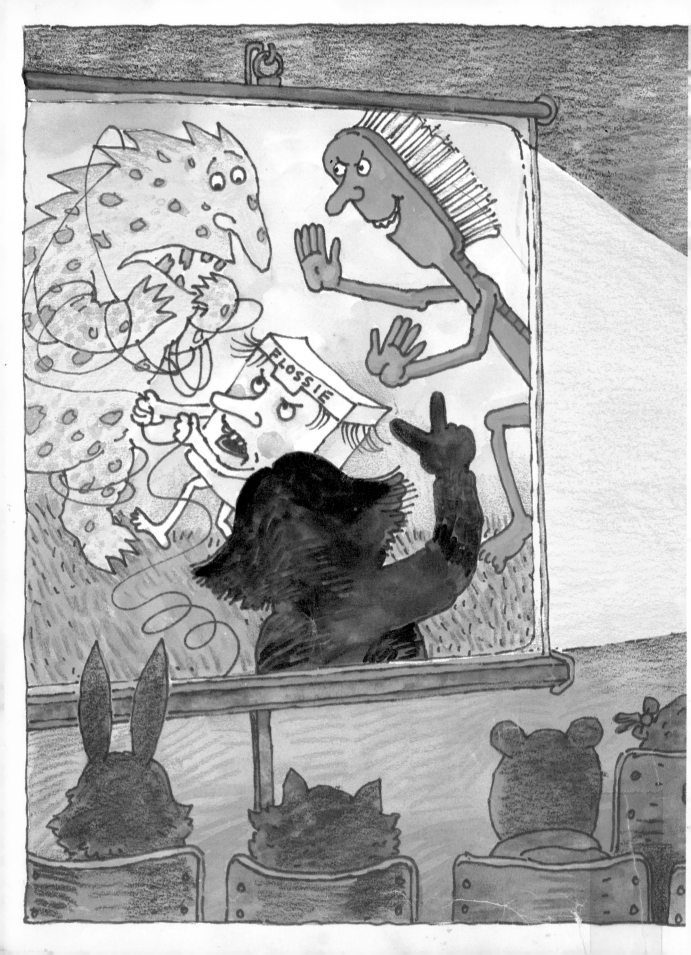

Later the class saw a movie
called *Nasty Mr. Tooth Decay.*
"Between the ages of four and seven,"
the announcer began, "everyone begins to lose
their deciduous, or baby, teeth."
"Everyone except Arthur!" shouted Francine.
The whole class laughed.
Arthur slid down in his seat. He wiggled his
tooth as hard as he could.

In the cafeteria, Francine practiced her new tricks.

"Look!" she said. "I can keep my teeth closed, and still drink through a straw. And I can squirt water, too. Everybody line up for a squirting contest — everybody except Arthur. Babies with baby teeth can't squirt water."

By the next day, Arthur was convinced his loose
tooth would never fall out.
His friends tried to help.
Buster brought carrots
for Arthur's lunch.

Sue Ellen showed Arthur how to put raisins over his
teeth to make it look as if some were missing.

The Brain invented a special machine.
"It's a tooth remover," he explained.
"Just put your head in here."

Even Binky Barnes wanted to help.
"I can knock that tooth out in one second flat," he said.

That night Arthur spent a lot of time in front of
the bathroom mirror.

He got up very early the next morning
to wiggle his tooth again.
"See how much looser it is!"
he told his parents.
"That's it," said his mother.
"You need professional help.
You're going to the dentist.
Today."

"Going to the dentist?" asked Francine.
"Boy, do I feel sorry for you!"

20

There were other patients waiting to see
Dr. Sozio.
"Sorry," said the nurse. "We're running late.
Have a seat."
"Arthur, you were smart to bring a book,"
said Mother.

Finally it was Arthur's turn.

"I wish all my patients were as good at waiting as you are," said Dr. Sozio. "How old are you now, Arthur?"

"Seven," said Arthur. "And I still have all my baby teeth."

"I was eight before I lost my first tooth," said Dr. Sozio. "Everyone is different."

"Really?" said Arthur.

Dr. Sozio examined Arthur's loose tooth.

"This one should fall out very soon," he said. "Just wait."

STERILIZER

EAT BALANCED MEALS

AND HEALTHY SNACKS

PADS

25

Arthur got back to school just in time for recess. "Still have all your baby teeth?" Francine asked. "Then you can't be in the game. I'm the tooth fairy. Only people who have lost teeth can play."

"If you're the tooth fairy," said Arthur,
"I think I'll keep all my teeth. I can wait."
He started over to the softball game.

"Whoever I touch," said Francine, "loses a tooth."
She flapped her arms.
"The one who loses the most, wins."

Francine twirled around and touched Buster.

She twirled faster, and touched Sue Ellen.

Twirling even faster, she slipped and hit Arthur.
"Sorry, Arthur," Francine said. "But I told you,
no babies allowed."

Arthur picked up his glasses.
"It's OK," he said. "It's probably the nicest
thing you've ever done for me."
"What do you mean?" asked Francine.

Arthur just smiled.